THE MERMAIDS & THE SEA MANATEES

FORM THEIR FIRST OCEAN SCHOOL

GARF.ORG 2021

SALLY JO HEADLEE

AuthorHouse™
1663 Liberty Drive
Bloomington, IN 47403
www.authorhouse.com
Phone: 833-262-8899

This book is printed on acid-free paper.

ISBN: 978-1-6655-3759-9 (sc)
ISBN: 978-1-6655-3760-5 (e)

Print information available on the last page.

Published by AuthorHouse 09/09/2021

authorHOUSE®

ATTENTION: ALL THE CREATURES FOUND LIVING IN OUR OUTDOOR ENVIRONMENTS. WE ARE INVITING YOU TO GO TO SCHOOL AND EDUCATE OTHERS ABOUT OUR STUGGLE FOR SUSTAINMENT IN NATURE.

Once upon a time, from a land far away, a family of ancient Sea Manatees met their land and Sea sisters the alluring human like mermaids.

When these two met they decided they had a, important story to share. As they spent hours sharing stories their Grandparents had shared with them. It did not take long before they realized that they had a compelling history that needed to be passed on to everyone who was willing to listen.

With the mighty wisdom of the manatees and the ever so enduring hearts of the mermaids, they decided to join–together to take you on a magical ride exploring through the vastness of our oceans, the rainforests, the wetlands, and field trips around the World to share their passion for the environment. They will share information regarding the possibilities and hope we desperately need to educate others about Mother Nature and the environment that sustains us. It is their compassion that they want you to share with your own Grandchildren, so these stories will be kept alive for generations to come.

At Children's bedtime so many untold miracles unfold. This is where Grandmothers meet with their beloved Grandchildren and tell stories that their own Grandparents shared with them. They speak of the history of the Ocean and all the interactions between fish, plant, corals, turtles and all the life that re–sides under the clear blue waters.

CHLOE THE MOST BEAUTIFUL MERMAID

As the Grandmothers tell the stories they highlight some of their own dreams to help preserve the interlocking relationships in our oceans. Never forgetting to embrace their continued hopes to explore even more treasures yet undiscovered.

As Molly the Grandmother was almost at the end of her story Mikie the manatee, eyes were getting heavy, and it was not long before he was dreaming of finding pearls and meeting Oliver the oyster.

You see Molly and Mikie have a special bond. For Mikie her Grandson was only six months old when he saved her from being captured in the fishing nets his parent where trapped in. This BIG boat sped off with Mikies parents, yet Molly vowed to make Mikies life as blessed as her was.

For she understood how Mikie felt for she lost her beloved husband the same way as he was captured in a net never to be seen again.

When Mikie was old enough Molly the Grandmother Manatee convinced Mikie that since the Ocean is full of so many schools of fish, we need to establish our own school. Our school, the lessons learned will be like planting little seeds in a garden, for our oceans need so much nurturing too.

MIKIE SCREAMED "CAN WE INVITE EVERYONE". As he took in a deep breath for, he had so much to say. Let us invite the land mermaids so they can help tell stories as they are one of the true ambassadors on land. We need to invite the fish, the turtles, the sea stars, the urchins, the sharks, heck, Grandmother Molly LET US INVITE EVERYONE!!

MIKIE AND OLIVER THE OYSTER

Molly and Mikie went out in the ocean searching for the perfect rocks to write on so they could announce the opening of this very special new school. It did not take long before they captured the attention of several sea creatures who promised to spread the word. They finished painting the signs with the time, date, and location of the classroom.

Molly looked down at her Grandson and expressed how proud she was of him. For education is so important for the ocean and its future.

In no time at all the first classroom of new students dedicated to learning about the ocean will be in session. So much positive energy will be everywhere. The school bell will ring in the dawn of a new day. With the mission to educate all creatures young and old.

Oh, Molly could already feel the passion spilling out of our oceans. With the hopes of creating waves knowledge and passion, until it reaches every single plant, animal, and human being.

This school, the lesson taught, and the messages presented are extremely important. It is critical we share facts about what the environment is suffering from and to provide the students with the tools they can use to help us keep the environment in balance and thriving.

It was a long day for both Molly and Mikie, each was exhausted, but that did not stop Molly from sharing yet another story with Mikie at bedtime. At the end of her story, she asked Mikie if he could think of ways to help save our wild resources that truly sustain so many lives

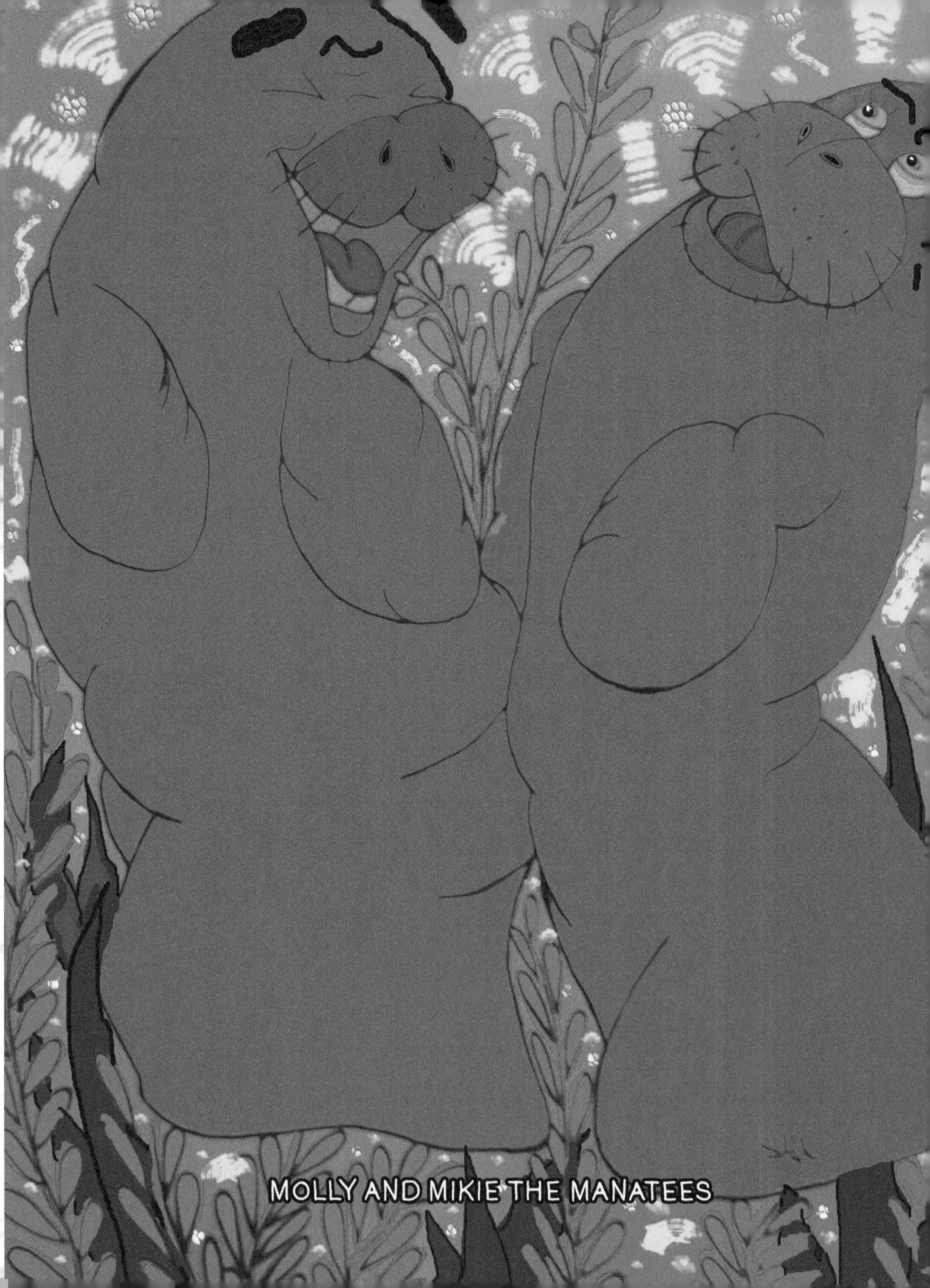
MOLLY AND MIKIE THE MANATEES

Mikie sat up in excitement and said I have several ideas.

We should turn off all the electrical items when we are not using them (if we are not allowed to turn them off, we could always remind our parents). Shut off lights when we are not in the room.

We could walk, ride a bike, or car–pool with someone, or ask our parents to (at least once a week).

When visiting the ocean, if you put on sunscreen, do not go into the water because the oils and chemicals can kill so many animals.

Tell your friends about the ocean. Inform them that coral is alive, that they are animals and that they desperately need us to be their voice.

Visit your Grandparents favorite fishing places and learn about the habitats they live in. Share your compassion for the ocean and the amazing creatures that live among us.

People will learn from you, and through your love they will begin to understand, they will begin to care about the ocean environment.

This is when Grandmother Molly screamed with excitement. She told Mikie to please save all this knowledge for tomorrow's first day of school. Mikie pinched himself just to make sure his excitement was not just a dream.

Soon Mikie fell fast asleep, as his dreams took him to so many of the schools of fish he visited while he played in freshwater or entered the salty sea waters of the ocean. In his dreams he took mental notes of the lessons shared so that he could pass them on to his new classmates he would meet in the morning.

STUDENTS ARE EXCITED FOR SCHOOL TO START

As all the new students entered the classroom, they quickly took their assigned seats for the day's lessons. Chloe, the youngest and most beautiful mermaid, asked her teacher this question, "What is wrong with the Worlds ocean's?"

The teacher, Miss Molly, the manatee, took in a deep breath and explained to Chloe that her question was very important, and that it was a question to which we do not have all the answers yet.

Miss Molly went on to say, "when we want to find the answers, we need to know some of the facts". More than ¾ of our planet is covered by water. However only 1% of that is actual made up of coral reefs and more than 50% of that tiny 1% is dead today. This means the loss of so many animals, so many of the homes, or the habitats they provided for our beloved fish and other animals.

So many factors are involved with the death and destruction of our oceans and their coral reefs. The first concern is with pollution. We have destroyed many of the wetlands that were the vital filter systems. Their root systems removed many of the toxicants now reaching from our rivers, lakes and flowing into our mighty oceans.

So many humans are building new homes, visiting resorts, and building even bigger businesses. These things combined cause immense stress on our oceans and the habitat it creates.

We have terrible fishing practices among the worst are bombing the reefs to catch fish or using poison.

Many Hotels and Resorts and golf courses are dumping sewage and countless chemicals into the oceans.

THE FIRST DAY OF SCHOOL

But one of the most critical stresses we are confronting is the increase in water temperatures. Elevated temperature makes the chemicals in the ocean water that much more potent.

Amity, the sea turtle, raised her head out of her shell as far as she could. She started to bounce her head up and down signaling that she had something important to say.

Miss Molly called on Amity to share her message. Amity explained that she had a personal story to tell. Amity turned to her classmates and told them about her Grandmother and Grandpa, who lived to be over 100 years old. She told them that her Grandparents drew a map and carefully placed it in a treasure chest. It showed all the wonderful healthy sea grass gardens where her Grandparents had feasted with all their friends and family.

Sadly, Amity reported that most of the gardens are gone now and that the ones that are left are struggling to survive and are no longer safe to eat.

The sea grasses that filter out the horrible chemicals are now found to have the chemicals in the stems of the grasses we used to consume. For the root systems of the sea grasses filter the water and absorb the chemicals, which makes them toxic to eat. They make her family sick and now many of her turtle cousins are being born deformed. Her own family is not living long as her past ancestors. So many of the stories from past generations are being lost forever. These stories are so important for they tell us where to find the best places to raise our families, what to eat, and teach our own children.

AMITY THE SEA TURTLE

Amity, then looked at her teacher Miss Molly, and smiled. Amities tears of the past were replaced with a faint smile as she shared the fact that several humans were now educating others about their habitats. These humans are learning how to breed and raise her cousins in captivity and releasing them into restored sea grass beds that are protected. She ended with the thought that there is always hope for all of us if we educate each other and work together.

It was at this time a young fish raised one of his little, wet, fins and said, "Teacher, I mean Miss Molly, what can we do to help save our environment?"

This is when the teacher Miss Molly reached out to all the students in her classroom, and she told them each to take the hands of the classmate that is next to them. She told them that they all have a role to play as today's pioneers.

For there is no way that one animal or human can do this alone. Simply stated, if we all do one simple caring thing we can, we must, save our ocean, that we all call home.

Miss Molly went on to explain that the ocean animals are some of the oldest life forms in the World.

There are so many incredible stories of our Grandparents journey that they used to share and pass on to the next generation. We must continue to pass them on in any way we can.

For it is through these very lessons and life experiences we can grow, not repeat mistakes of the past, and we can develop new sustainable ways to face all the new challenges that come our way.

MISS MOLLY'S PASSION FOR THE OCEAN IS REAL

Miss Molly stood up real tall and said, we took one of the most important steps today. Inviting all of you to this new school. Having the mermaids in class is critical so they can take the story all over the land to educate humans. The mermaids can explain to them that it is not what is being taken out of the oceans that is killing the life within the ocean water, but it is clearly what is going in. From one lake, to our rivers all water flows into our ocean.

Miss Molly asked them to grab the piece of paper and pencil on each of their desks. She explained I want you to write down these things, these simple, yet effective things we can ask your parents to do. You can help them and remind them of these important tasks, as we all set examples for the rest of the life in the ocean.

Let us start by writing down the positive changes we can make to help save our damaged environment.

We should be careful what we throw away in our trash. We should recycle when at all possible. Ask our leaders to make sure there are rules and regulations about what can and cannot be dumped to close to any water source.

Research safe ways to dispose of plastics and try and avoid using more than necessary.

We all need to remember not to put tons of sunscreen on before swimming. Once we are done playing in the water and we want to protect ourselves from the sun we can place the sunscreen on us but do not go back in the water. Make certain the bottle is not laying in the sand, so the mighty tide does not carry it into the ocean. If the bottle is empty, make sure to dispose of it properly.

SHARE YOUR PASSION ABOUT THE ENVIRONMENT

Share what you know about our few natural wetlands that are left, explain how it is such a vital filter keeping so many of the chemicals away from our water playgrounds. We can not destroy one more of them.

If you think about what happens when you build a golf course to close to any river, or a lake or a resort. Everything they do to keep the grass green is accomplished through chemicals. Often those chemicals and grass clippings end up in the ponds that are blanketed throughout the course. When this happens, the ponds grow algae and the golf courses end up using even more, chemicals that they pour directly into their ponds to try and get rid of the algae. We can learn and teach others how to grow plants that will filter the water. This would create jobs and help clean up the environment all at the same time.

We need to teach ourselves and others how to fish properly so there is no more poison, or bombing, or illegal fishing. We can use nets, which can create income as some of the animals would need to make them and fix them when they break.

Miss Molly added with great pride, my Grandson Mikie suggested last night that we can walk, ride a bike, ask to ride with a friend by car–pooling. This will make a HUGE difference in how much of the green–houses gases are released into our air.

Your homework assignment is to write down more methods we should practice that would help save our Worlds ocean. For as we all work together there is hope for the life that sustains us all.

TOGETHER WE CAN AND WILL MAKE A DIFFERENCE

These simple changes may take time however they will safeguard our oceans for future generations. We need to listen to our Grandparents stories as they share their time spent in our Oceans. We need to remember and repeat these same stories as well as the ones yet to come so that no history is lost between generations.

Humans can share stories of their favorite fishing places. They can show pictures of the fish and ocean creatures they met.

In the ocean we will be sharing stories of the new reef communities being built and new species being uncovered. Oh, and let us not forget about that constant search for that treasure chest still left undiscovered.

At this time, the school bell rang, and the students swam as fast as they could. They were so excited to tell Mommy and Daddy what they learned in school today. They were even more anxious for bedtime as new stories will be shared by their Grandparents as they alertly listen to every word.

Finally, with the little energy left within them their hearts and their minds were full of visions and desires, that as today's pioneers they could soon roll up their fins and help save the wild reefs even if for now it would have to be a task for many tomorrows.

In no time at all their first homework assignment was completed.

At the end of their day Grandmother told them their bedtime story. They fell fast asleep dreaming of the school field trips yet to come.

THE END

What can you do to help the Sea Manatee's and Ocean School educate others about the future of our beloved ocean?

List the things that you will do to help protect the ocean for generations to come.

1.

2.

3.

4.

Draw some of your favorite sea creatures.

WATCH FOR BOOK TWO–AS THE MANATEE AND OCEAN SCHOOL TAKE THEIR FIRST FIELD TRIP LEARNING ABOUT THE WORLDS HABITATS.

WITH PASSION FOR THE ENVIRONMENT THAT SUSTAINS US THERE IS HOPE FOR OUR FUTURE PLANET.

Sally Jo Headlee—2021 Acknowledgements

It would take me so many pages of so many books to define all the people who guided me on my journey in life. I first must mention my beloved husband LeRoy Headlee who passed away in 2012. I was the Executive Director for the Idaho Botanical Gardens when I met LeRoy. LeRoy would spend countless hours volunteering his time working on the Garden's pond. We would spend time sharing our passion for the environment. His passion was for everything wet, my passion was for everything alive. That combo together could be and never will be shadowed by any other event in my lifetime It was LeRoy who gifted me my first empty tank. What a journey it has been. Many of these stories along the way will be shared throughout these series of Children's books. Taking you on natures field trips exploring so many of the blessings far too many of us simply take for granted. Next, I must mention my Daughter Misty Dawn Rogers who helped fuel my passion for animals and the habitats that sustain them. My Daughter blessed my life with two of the most precious Granddaughters any Grandmother could hope for. My first Granddaughter's name is Chloe who is one of the key students in all the books. Chloe is the most beautiful mermaid in the World she has not only continued to live up to this title she does it with her outward stunning beauty and a spirit of light, warmth, grace, and such passion within her. My second Granddaughter's name is Amity. She is also mentioned in each book and plays a critical role in bringing each book to life. Amity is the ever so curious sea turtle who always brings up food. Amity's favorite subject was food. I do not think there was any food that she was afraid to sample and some of her facial expressions were priceless. So, on each field trip the creatures go on watch for Amity to bring up something about food. Next, I must, I simply can not forget to mention my own Grandmother who was the best storyteller of all times. I come from a family of five children and as we would visit our Grandmother when it was bedtime, she would have us all sit around one bed and say pick a word. Any word. Each one of us would think of a word that in no way could ever match or fit into one story. Once she had every one's assigned word, she would begin telling her story. As she went along in the story somehow, some magical way she would make each word fit into the story and giggle when we realized she added our word into the story. Her ability to weave any story together from any words I believe is what gifted me with my ability to be the voice for the animals that simply own my soul. I can only hope that in some small way that my Grandmother Vickers is as proud of me as I am of her. My final acknowledgement is to Doctor Christopher Davidson. He is my Hero for at some of the most painful and dark times of my life his light always shined. He saw in me what I did not, he polished me so that I would shine in all that I do and all that I touch. One of my favorite statements he has repeated often, that just tickles me every time I hear it is "don't ever tell Sally Jo she cannot do something for she will find a way." He is my mentor, my best Friend and so special beyond words. He helped with editing these books but for the spelling errors, or backward sentences they are all my doing. I just know inside of me I have so many stores to share and have promised the animals that carry my being that while there is a breath left inside of me, I will be their voice. Sally Jo Headlee

CPSIA information can be obtained
at www.ICGtesting.com
Printed in the USA
LVHW071940290921
699022LV00008B/105